WHOOSH and CHUG!

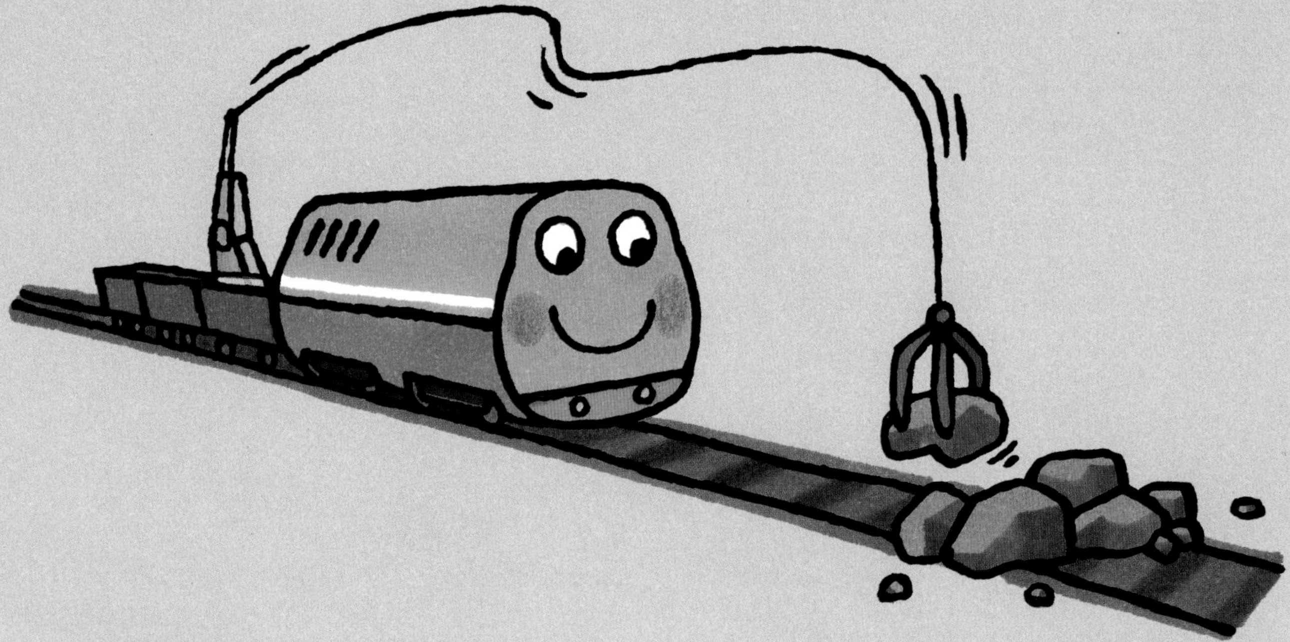

For Oscar and Leo — S.B.

Whoosh and Chug!
Copyright © 2012 by Sebastien Braun
All rights reserved. Manufactured in China.

iSBN 978-0-06-207754-7 (trade bdg.)

The artist used india ink outline with a marker fill to create the digital illustrations for this book.
Title Design by Rachel Zegar
14 15 16 17 18   SCP   10 9 8 7 6 5 4 3 2 1
❖
First U.S. edition, 2014
Originally published in Great Britain by HarperCollins Children's Books in 2012.

WHOOSH and CHUG!

by Sebastien Braun

HARPER
An Imprint of HarperCollinsPublishers

CHUG!

CHUG!

CHUG!

This is Chug. Hello, Chug!
He is a very busy little engine.

Every day Chug works hard collecting
and delivering heavy freight.

CHUG!

CHUG!

CHUG!

He might be slow, but he is very careful.

One morning, while the other trains were still asleep, Chug had to set off early for work.

CHUG!

CHUG!

CHUG!

Whoosh, the passenger train, opened his eyes. "Catch you later, slowpoke!" he called out.

Chug went slowly on his way,
into the forest . . .

past the lake . . .

and through the tunnel.

He stopped at the station to make
a delivery, and then he went on.

CHUG!

CHUG!

CHUG!

Eventually Chug
reached the junction.

"Stop!"

cried Sigmund, the signal box.
"There's danger on the line ahead.
Wait for the green light; then you
can move on to the safe track."

So Chug waited . . .

and waited . . .

but still the light didn't
change to green.

Suddenly . . .

osh!

"Slowpoke! I *knew* I'd beat you!"
laughed Whoosh, hurtling down
the track toward the canyon.
"STOP!" shouted Chug. "It's not safe!"

But it was too late. . . .

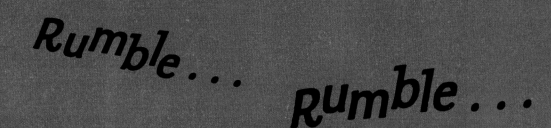

Rumble... Rumble... Rumble...

As Whoosh sped along, he heard the
rocks begin to creak and groan . . .

and then they tumbled
down the canyon.

CRASH!

CRASH!

Whoosh kept going as
the rocks smashed onto the
track behind him, until . . .

Chug was still waiting at the light
when he heard Whoosh calling out.
"I'm coming!" he yelled back.

Chug bravely made his way down the dangerous track toward the cries for help.

Using his crane, he cleared
the rocks off the track,

slowly and carefully,

one by one,

until his freight cars were
completely full . . .

and Whoosh was free at last!

"Thank you, Chug. I was *so* scared," said Whoosh, reversing down the track.

Together the two friends started to make their way back home.

"You must be more careful next time, Whoosh," said Sigmund as they passed by. "We don't want any accidents."

"I promise," said Whoosh.

"Thank you for being such a good friend," said Whoosh, once they were safely settled in the sidings. "You might have to work slowly, but you are very quick to come to the rescue!"

Chug smiled at Whoosh. . . .

"It's all in a day's work," he said.